SO-BOS-899

Raise the Roof!

WNBA Superstars

BY MICHELLE SMITH

SCHOLASTIC INC.
New York   Toronto   London   Auckland   Sydney
Mexico City   New Delhi   Hong Kong

To Jerry

PHOTO CREDITS
NBA Entertainment Photos

Cover (Griffith), Back cover (Staley), 24, 71: Rocky Widner. **Cover (Smith), 91:** Norm Perdue. **Cover (Thompson):** Paul Chapman. **Back cover (Weatherspoon), 36, 76, 83:** Nathaniel S. Butler. **4, 46, 51, 53:** David Sherman. **6, 56, 61:** Garrett Ellwood. **8:** Allen Einstein. **11:** Don Grayston. **18:** Jose Luis Villegas. **21:** Mitchell Layton. **28:** Barry Gossage. **31:** Andrew D. Bernstein. **41:** Gary Bassing. **66:** Kent Smith. **73:** Bill Baptist. **80:** Ray Amati. **86:** Scott Troyanos.

PHOTO CREDITS: INSERT SECTION
NBA Entertainment Photos

I, VII: Norm Perdue. **II:** Rocky Widner. **III:** Andrew D. Bernstein. **IV:** Fernando Medina. **V (left):** David Sherman. **V (right):** Kent Smith. **VI:** Nathaniel S. Butler. **VIII:** Bill Baptist.

ISBN 0-439-24112-X

Copyright © 2001 by WNBA Enterprises, LLC
All rights reserved. Published by Scholastic Inc.

SCHOLASTIC and associated logos are trademarks and/or registered trademarks of Scholastic Inc.

12 11 10 9 8 7 6 5 4 3 2 1   1 2 3 4 5 6 / 0

Printed in the U.S.A.
First Scholastic printing, June 2001
Book Design: Michael Malone

TABLE OF CONTENTS

INTRODUCTION

Katie Smith

Across the country, Jennifer Azzi, Natalie Williams and Teresa Weatherspoon burst forth from posters that are tacked to thousands of bedroom walls. Girls in jerseys with *Griffith* and *Thompson* striped across the back flock to arenas all over the U.S., ready to cheer their heroes.

The WNBA has not only created a place for the best women's basketball players in the world to come together and show their stuff, but it has also become a place for girls to find their inspiration and role models.

It wasn't always that way.

Five years ago, the WNBA wasn't a thriving professional sports league with big-time players, sponsors and TV deals. It was just an idea. An idea that many people weren't sure would ever work. After all, 13 U.S. women's professional basketball leagues had come before, and all of them had failed.

But the WNBA is still here and it's going strong.

In 2001, the WNBA will be in its fifth season, proving all doubters wrong—it's a complete success! The league has experienced tremendous growth. Millions of fans have attended WNBA games, and tens of millions more have watched games on television. National sponsors have signed on, and the league has gone from just eight teams, way back in 1997, to 16 teams in the 2000 season.

The level of basketball is better than ever. When the American Basketball League folded in 1998, that league's top players joined the teams in the WNBA and propelled their squads to new levels of success.

Dawn Staley

Now, WNBA rosters are stacked with the best women basketball players in the world. They are not just the American stars—many of whom braved homesickness and new languages to play overseas for many years—but they are also star players from Portugal, Poland, Australia, Russia, Brazil and many more countries.

At the dawn of the new millennium, the WNBA's biggest names—Lisa Leslie, Sheryl Swoopes and Nikki McCray—are joined by a growing list of players whose names are becoming as big as their games—players like Dawn Staley, Katie Smith, DeLisha Milton and Nykesha Sales.

Women have been playing basketball since the late 19th century. They are playing it better than ever in the 21st. The future of the WNBA is bright because many of the same girls who are watching and marveling at their heroes on the court today may be taking their places on the court someday in the future. But now, let's celebrate today's stars....

Jennifer Azzi

If there is a living example of the saying "practice makes perfect," it might just be Jennifer Azzi. In Jennifer's mind, there is always work to be done.

That is why she shoots baskets and shags her own rebounds long after her teammates have gone home for the day, sometimes after they have gone to bed.

That is why she runs three miles on the treadmill every day and then throws in some sprints, just for the extra workout.

That is why she lifts weights until the perfectly defined muscles in her arms and legs glisten with sweat.

These are the reasons why she is one of the best, most respected basketball players on the planet. The Utah Starzz veteran point guard has a reputation for being a tireless worker and a passionate competitor. She is the kind of player who, according to her college and Olympic team coach, Tara VanDerveer, can take a team "from the basement to the penthouse."

Her coach would know. She has won an NCAA title and an Olympic gold medal thanks to Jennifer's sharp shooting and leadership on her teams.

Jennifer once said, "I wasn't born great. I was born with some abilities like running and jumping." But she wouldn't be able to find the rim with her eyes closed or make a left-handed layup without a lot of hard work as well.

Jennifer's natural abilities began to show themselves early, when she was a kid in Oak Ridge, Tennessee. In fact, she was just four years old.

Her mother, Donna, picked Jennifer up from nursery school one day when the teacher asked Mrs. Azzi to step outside. Donna walked out to the playground to see Jennifer tossing a basketball—overhand—into the basket.

Donna explained, "I said, 'Oh, wow, that was lucky,' and the teacher said, 'No, you don't understand, she's been doing that all morning.'"

From then on, it proved difficult to get Jennifer to stop playing ball. She played her first organized game in the first grade. It was called "Bitty Ball," and was played with a small ball and eight-foot baskets. Jennifer can still remember the excitement of her first game. She started getting ready at eight in the morning.

Jennifer's enthusiasm showed no matter what sport she played. "Whatever sport I was playing was my favorite sport at the time," Jennifer said. "If it was softball, then I would be sitting in my uniform at ten A.M. for a six o'clock game. I would drive everyone crazy."

In addition to basketball and softball, Jennifer played soccer, ran cross-country and track, competing in the hurdles, the long jump and the high jump.

Yet basketball, somehow, seemed to be the sport she loved the most. Her mother would have to walk down to the school gym and call her by her full name—"Jennifer Lynn Azzi!"—to get her to come home for dinner.

It didn't occur to Jennifer that she might continue playing basketball in college until the summer before her junior year, when she played well in a big tournament and started to be showered with letters from coaches and recruiters.

But Jennifer told her high school coach she didn't want to play in college. "I thought I wanted to be a normal person," Jennifer explained. "There was only so much girls could do with basketball back then."

But it was clear Jennifer could do quite a bit. She led Oak Ridge High to a 34–2 record in her senior season, helping her team reach the state finals. She was named the East Tennessee Player of the Year.

Top colleges such as Maryland, Ohio State, Stanford and Vanderbilt were all interested in Jennifer. She decided to take a chance on Stanford, which had a great academic reputation but had not yet built itself into a national basketball power. In fact, the crowds were so small in coach Tara VanDerveer's first season in 1985 that most of the bleachers didn't even need to be pulled out. Jennifer's arrival in 1986 changed all that.

Jennifer has called it a "gut feeling" that she chose Stanford. "It was the only place I really wanted to go." She had the feeling something special would happen at Stanford, and she was right!

If Jennifer had a tough time adjusting to college basketball and her new home in California, it rarely showed. She was too busy training for the season. It was the usual exhausting combination of weight-lifting, running and shooting.

Some nights, she and teammate Sonja Henning would play midnight pickup games with the guys in the Stanford gym. The work paid off. Jennifer led Stanford to a 101–23 record in her four-year career. The team played in three NCAA Tournaments and in 1990 won the NCAA Championship. That same season, Jennifer was named the National Player of the Year.

Unfortunately, there was no professional league in the U.S., so Jennifer followed many of her talented peers to Europe, where American players are not only paid well, but are treated like celebrities.

But that was a difficult life. Jennifer spent hundreds of dollars every month on phone bills and wished she were back in the States. When she came home she felt discouraged when people would ask her what she was doing with her life. When she said she was playing basketball, they would look confused. No one in the States knew that there was a professional women's basketball league thousands of miles away in Europe.

Jennifer competed for teams in Italy, France and Sweden, and barely missed making the 1992 Olympic team. When the opportunity to try out for the Olympic team came around again in 1996, Jennifer seized it. She earned her spot on the U.S. team under the watchful eye of her old coach, Tara VanDerveer.

"That whole year and a half preparing for the Olympics was such an amazing experience," Jennifer said. She traveled all over the world with the U.S. team in preparation for the Olympics and became one of the team's most recognizable players, appearing in television commercials and in national magazines. But when the team arrived in Atlanta for the Olympics, there was nothing to think about but basketball.

Jennifer was a bundle of nerves. On the morning of the team's first game, Jennifer sat with her teammates at breakfast. No one was eating.

Jennifer hadn't slept the night before.

The U.S. team won that game, and every other one they played on the way to the gold medal. Jennifer celebrated the team's gold-medal victory over Brazil by doing cartwheels on the court.

The attention received by women's basketball during the Olympic Games resulted in the formation of two women's professional leagues in the United States. For Jennifer, it was a dream come true: a chance to play at home. She began playing in the American Basketball League (ABL) in the fall of 1996 for the San Jose Lasers, just miles from where she became a basketball star at Stanford.

Two years later, Jennifer was devastated when the ABL folded. It was one of the most difficult things she'd ever faced. She wasn't sure she wanted to play anymore. But after a lot of thought she decided she would continue her career in the WNBA and was taken by the Detroit Shock in the 1999 WNBA Draft.

Jennifer considered retiring from the game after the 1999 season. She spent the off-season away from basketball, running training camps in the Bay Area of California. But she missed the game too much. She wanted to play.

Jennifer was traded to the Utah Starzz before the 2000 season began. Then Jennifer broke her hand during training camp and missed the first five weeks of the season.

She finally came back on July 7. And she was nervous. "I still get nervous before games. Not scared, just nervous," Jennifer said. "I don't know what it is. But I think if I didn't [get nervous], it would be bad."

That's the same way Jennifer feels about all that practice. It pays off.

Jennifer Azzi

Position	Height	Weight	Birth Date	College
Guard	5-8	147	8/31/68	Stanford '90

Season	Team	G	FG%	FT%	3P%	APG	RPG	SPG	BPG	PPG	PTS
1999	Detroit	28	.514	.827	.517	3.8	2.2	.86	.14	10.8	302
2000	Utah	15	.452	.930	.417	6.1	2.7	.80	.33	9.6	144
Career		43	.491	.857	.488	4.6	2.4	.84	.21	10.4	446

Did you know
that Jennifer runs her own
basketball training camps for kids in
the San Francisco Bay Area?

Yolanda Griffith

Before every game, Yolanda and Candace Griffith have a pregame ritual.

Candace sits in the row behind the Sacramento Monarchs' bench. As the lineups are announced, Yolanda turns and hands Candace, her 11-year-old daughter, her gold chain. Then she kisses Candace on the forehead and heads off into the basketball battle.

As anyone who has ever played against Yolanda knows, that's all the time it takes for the Sacramento Monarchs star center to turn from loving, devoted mother into one of the game's fiercest competitors.

The WNBA's 1999 Most Valuable Player is an impressive combination of athletic talents. Her speed and agility are unmatched for a player her size (6-4). "Yo," as she is known, has large hands and quick feet, which means she rarely loses the battle for a rebound. And somehow, it seems, she is everywhere. Under the basket waiting for the pass. Along the sideline waiting for the chance to make the steal.

"To me, Yolanda is the best player in the WNBA," said former Detroit Shock coach Nancy Lieberman-Cline, a member of the Basketball Hall of Fame. "Yolanda is the best big player in the world."

Yolanda has worked as hard at motherhood as she

has at basketball. Together Yolanda and Candace have lived through all the ups and downs of Mom's career from the time that Candace was just a baby.

"God has blessed me with a beautiful daughter and I want Candace to count on me," Yolanda said. "It's been hard getting from when she was born to where we are now. I've had a lot of support. My family has been right there in my corner. I have no regrets."

Yolanda knows about being a single parent all too well. She watched her father, Harvey, raise five children after Yolanda's mother died suddenly when Yolanda was just 13 years old. Yolanda, the youngest child, tried to remember a lesson her mother had taught her to get through her grief: "Where there's darkness, there's always a bright side."

Yolanda created her bright side with a stellar high school sports career. She was an All-American in basketball and softball at Chicago's George Washington Carver High School.

Basketball had been an outlet for Yolanda's energy for a long time. She'd been playing since she was six years old, starting at the grammar school playground across the street from her house.

"My mom and dad got me a ball and said they would watch me," Yolanda said. "They were trying

to keep me out of trouble." Yolanda would play while her parents sat on the porch. She did not play organized basketball until she was in eighth grade, when she was put on an all-boys team. At first she was nervous. The boys did their best to push her around, but she was bigger than them!

Her entire family was thrilled when she was recruited by the University of Iowa, one of the top women's basketball programs in the country. She headed to Iowa to begin her college career. But she never played a game there.

Before the season began, Yolanda found out she was pregnant.

"The first thing that crossed my mind was 'How am I going to tell everyone?' I was scared," Yolanda said. "Everybody had such high hopes for me. We all had so many goals and I felt like I let everybody down."

In fact, her father and her brothers and sisters took the news hard. But Yolanda decided the best thing was to move home and raise her child with the help of her family.

After Candace was born, Yolanda and her baby stayed in Chicago for a year. During that time, Yolanda decided she not only wanted to play basketball again, but she wanted to get an education, too. So she put her daughter in the car and they drove more than a thousand miles to Florida, where Yolanda played at Palm Beach Junior College for two years, earning Junior College All-American honors. She obviously still had plenty of game.

Those were not easy times. Yolanda couldn't afford to eat much more than Ramen noodles and she had to take a job repossessing cars from people who owed money. It was dangerous work. Yolanda would often work at night, hot-wiring cars before the owner realized what was going on.

"You do what you have to do," recalled Yolanda. "I never had anyone pull a gun on me. That always happened to my boss."

Finally, big-time college programs came calling again. But Yolanda was thinking of her daughter's best interests. Instead of Tennessee, Yolanda chose Florida Atlantic, a small Division II college, because she didn't want to disrupt Candace's day-care routine.

After her junior season at Florida Atlantic, the phone rang. It was a professional team in Germany, offering Yolanda a basketball contract and a salary of $18,000. It was an offer that was too good to pass up. Yolanda boarded the plane without Candace. Three-year-old Candace came a month later with a family friend.

"It was very scary, going to a new place," Yolanda said. "I had no idea what it was going to be like."

Yolanda and Candace stayed in Germany for three years, learning the language and missing home. They returned to the United States when Candace said she was ready to come home.

It was the American Basketball League's second year. Yolanda signed a contract with them upon her return and became the surprise player of the year, finishing second in the MVP voting. Few had seen her combination of size and speed, power and grace.

A year later when the ABL folded, Yolanda moved to the WNBA, where she was taken by Sacramento as the second pick in the 1999 draft, behind Tennessee star Chamique Holdsclaw.

Yolanda's first season in the WNBA was more than she could have ever imagined. She helped the Sacramento Monarchs go from having one of the worst records in the league in 1998 to the playoffs in 1999. But the Monarchs struggled in the post-season, after Yolanda suffered a season-ending knee injury three games before the playoffs began.

By then, however, Yolanda had already been named the league's Most Valuable Player, its Defensive Player of the Year and its Newcomer of the Year. She led the WNBA in rebounding and steals and was second in scoring.

Despite the fact that mom and daughter are stable and comfortable, with no more overseas plane tickets and new languages to learn, Yolanda is still making choices with Candace's interests in mind. She missed a tryout for the U.S. Olympic team in 1998 because she didn't want to miss Candace's first day of school. She tried out a few months later and made the team. And of course, Candace was in Sydney watching her mother play for Team USA.

Yolanda hasn't had too many bad days in her career lately. But after a tough loss, she always turns to her daughter.

"She's so positive. I might have had the worst game of my life, but she will always come up to me and say 'Good game, Mom,'" Yolanda said. "I always say 'What did I tell you about lying to me?'"

When they leave the arena, Yolanda and Candace leave basketball behind.

"We go go-cart riding or to the movies," Yolanda said. "When I'm on the court, it's about me working hard and wanting to compete. When the game is over, it's all about doing what she wants."

It's always been that way.

Yolanda Griffith

Position	Height	Weight	Birth Date	College
Forward	6-4	175	3/1/70	Florida Atlantic '93

Season	Team	G	FG%	FT%	3P%	APG	RPG	SPG	BPG	PPG	PTS
1999	Sacramento	29	.541	.617	.000	1.6	11.3	2.52	1.86	18.8	545
2000	Sacramento	32	.535	.706	.000	1.5	10.3	2.59	1.91	16.3	523
Career		61	.538	.657	.000	1.5	10.8	2.56	1.89	17.5	1,068

Did you know

that Yolanda wants to work in law enforcement after her basketball career ends?

DeLisha Milton

DeLisha Milton was just 11 years old when something happened that changed her life. She was attending vacation Bible school when she slipped into a swimming pool and hit her head.

She fought hard to get to the surface and began swallowing water. DeLisha was in trouble. She was pulled from the pool and resuscitated. Ever since, people have told her that she was blessed and destined for a bright future.

One look at DeLisha's life as a professional basketball player and Olympian and it's hard to argue. DeLisha is a WNBA All-Star who plays for the Los Angeles Sparks and was a member of the gold medal-winning 2000 Olympic team in Sydney. She has a reputation as a fierce competitor. The 6-1 forward is an impressive combination of long limbs, wiry strength and nonstop intensity. And DeLisha loves defense.

She also has a reputation as one of the most giving, generous people her family, friends and teammates have ever known. That's why the people who know her call her "Sunshine." The "Sunshine" part of DeLisha has helped support family members, read books to elementary school kids, put a basketball hoop up at a battered women's shelter and supported numerous charity causes like breast cancer and Alzheimer's disease research.

"When you score thirty-five points, they might praise you for a week and then it's gone," DeLisha said. "When I go into the community, it's a lasting impression."

Then there's the part of DeLisha that Sparks coach Michael Cooper calls "D-Nasty." He gave her the nickname because of the way she competes on the basketball court.

"She is D-Nasty and she is Sunshine," Coach Cooper said. "She will smile at you while she gives you an elbow. There is a lot of energy and determination bundled up in that frame."

"When D-Nasty comes out, people are like 'What's wrong with you?'" DeLisha said with a smile. "And I tell them I'm not Miss Nice Girl all the time." Just about 95 percent of the time, she says. "I have a lot of things to be happy about."

DeLisha is a professional basketball star with an Olympic gold medal. The only thing she doesn't have is a lot of free time. DeLisha has been playing competitive basketball almost constantly since her college career ended in 1997. She rarely takes a break.

When DeLisha does get a chance to go home to Riceboro, Georgia, she relaxes in her own way. Her mother, Beverly, makes home-cooked seafood and DeLisha plays pickup basketball with her four cousins, Lewis, Jason, Jarvis and Elton Jr., who don't

RAISE THE ROOF!

take it easy on their famous cousin. They push, they defend, they block shots. It's part of what makes her so tough.

On Sunday afternoons she squeezes in a shoot-around, after spending the morning with her mother at First Zion Baptist Church.

Riceboro is a small town of 700 people. It is so small it has just two blinking yellow lights and no grocery store. But Riceboro is so proud of its local hero that it declared "DeLisha Milton Day" the day after DeLisha became a professional basketball player. It was a celebration that included banners, food and music. DeLisha was overwhelmed.

"The kids in this area always looked to her as a mentor," said DeLisha's uncle, Elton Brown Sr. There wasn't anybody in town who didn't know about the basketball star who earned a scholarship to the University of Florida. It wasn't a big surprise that DeLisha picked Florida, because her sister Charmaine was already there. And Florida was thrilled to have a player who was a two-time Naismith High School Player of the Year, in 1992 and 1993.

Florida coach Carol Ross knew she had more than a special player. She knew she had a special person as well. DeLisha would go into Coach Ross's office all the time. She would sit down in a chair in front of the coach's desk and they would talk. They would talk

Jennifer Azzi

Yolanda Griffith

DeLisha Milton

Dawn Staley

Katie
Smith

Teresa Weatherspoon

Natalie Williams

Tina Thompson

about school and basketball, and DeLisha would tell her coach how much she wanted to be an Olympian.

"Not only am I proud of where she has gone with her career, but how she's done it," said Coach Ross. "To see someone's dream become a reality—it's what every coach dreams of."

DeLisha helped lead Florida to the Elite Eight in the NCAA Tournament and became the only player in school history to win the Wade Trophy as the nation's outstanding senior in 1997. She holds school records for steals, games started and is fourth in scoring.

DeLisha was the second pick in the 1997 draft, selected by the Portland Power in the American Basketball League. Not only did she make Portland her home, but she made a home for her 18-year-old cousin Elton Jr., as well, who was struggling to stay out of trouble in Riceboro.

DeLisha and Elton lived together in her Portland apartment. She tried to teach him to be neat and helped him get part-time jobs. Meanwhile, she played basketball and proved to be an inspiration.

Elton's mother called DeLisha "the answer from God to my prayers."

DeLisha simply does what she thinks is right. DeLisha is known as a player with a big heart. It's what makes her such a great basketball talent despite the fact that she's usually smaller than most of the players she's guarding. Her 84-inch arm-span is equal to a player standing seven feet tall.

"The other players might be taller, but they are probably not faster than me," DeLisha said. "The more I get up and down the floor and keep them active, the quicker they are out of the game. I love it when I see that I'm wearing somebody down."

Twice in her professional career, DeLisha was good enough to be a first-round draft pick. After the ABL folded, DeLisha became the fourth overall selection in the 1999 WNBA Draft by the Los Angeles Sparks. She was thrilled at the prospect of playing side by side with Lisa Leslie, who is one of DeLisha's basketball heroes.

The two post players have made a dynamic combination, not only for the Sparks—who reached the playoffs for the second straight year in the 2000 season—but for the U.S. Olympic team as well. DeLisha was honored to have played with Leslie, five-time Olympian Teresa Edwards, Nikki McCray and Dawn Staley. It's hard for her to believe that she belongs among them.

One night, during the U.S. team's fall 1999 tour, DeLisha sat with her teammates in a hotel room. They were doing their usual things—playing cards, doing one another's hair, watching a movie—when

Lisa started telling stories about the 1996 Olympics.

"She talked about how hard it was, but also how fun it was," DeLisha said. "I want to be the one sitting there the next time. I want great basketball stories, too."

There is little doubt for anyone who knows her that she will have them.

DeLisha Milton

Position	Height	Weight	Birth Date	College
Forward	6-1	172	9/11/74	Florida '97

Season	Team	G	FG%	FT%	3P%	APG	RPG	SPG	BPG	PPG	PTS
1999	Los Angeles	32	.530	.791	.000	1.6	5.5	1.47	.53	9.9	318
2000	Los Angeles	32	.512	.745	.250	2.1	6.1	1.38	.91	11.8	378
Career		64	.520	.766	.222	1.8	5.8	1.42	.72	10.9	696

Did you know
that DeLisha has been known to trip over things that aren't even there?

Nykesha
Sales

No one knew it at the time, but the day when six-year-old Nykesha Sales went to visit her aunt and uncle was an important one.

Soon after she arrived, she headed outside in search of something to do. She found a basketball and a hoop nailed to the side of the apartment building. Nykesha began tossing the ball under-handed toward the rim. And then it went in!

Her uncle watched her for a while, and then showed her how to shoot an overhand shot. It was much harder. Her thin arms didn't seem strong enough to heave that heavy ball up to the rim.

"But I didn't want to stop," Nykesha said. "I just kept pushing it up there and pushing it up there." Finally, she scored!

As it turned out, her basketball accomplish-ments were only beginning. Twenty-four-year-old Nykesha is one of the WNBA's brightest young tal-ents, a two-time All-Star in just two seasons with the Orlando Miracle. She can score with the best players in the league, and is also known for her athleticism, her deft ball-handling and her tough defense.

Every girl has got to start somewhere. Once Nykesha mastered that overhand shot, she dis-covered there wasn't anywhere she could use her newfound talent. There were no basketball leagues for girls in her hometown of Bloomfield, Connecticut. On the playground at school, Nykesha would walk past the girls playing double Dutch and over to the concrete court, waiting and watching until the boys let her play.

Nykesha's love for the game grew strong.

"It got to the point where I was really upset if I couldn't play," Nykesha said. "That would always be my punishment when I did something wrong. My mom would say I couldn't go to the recreation center and shoot and I would be devastated. I would be in tears, begging her to let me go."

Nykesha's mom, Kim, encouraged her daughter's interest in sports. She signed Nykesha up for anything she wanted to play—soccer, baseball, volleyball. But there was a catch. She would have to bring her little brother, Brooks, with her.

"She'd sign me up for something and sign him up, too," Nykesha said. "And I'd have to drag him along."

Nykesha was in seventh grade when she was invited by the junior high athletic director to play on a boys' traveling team. She wasn't sure she could do it.

"But the guys I grew up with told me I could play," Nykesha said. "People told me since I was a girl I couldn't compete, but I proved them wrong."

.

It wasn't until the next year that she finally got to play on a girls' team. The track coach brought her a brochure about a local Amateur Athletic Union (AAU) team for girls. He told her she was good enough to go to the tryout. When she got to the gym, it was filled with girls. She didn't realize there were this many girls playing basketball like her. She was thrilled!

Playing with the AAU team took her out of Connecticut for the first time in her life. She went to places like Washington, D.C.; Louisiana; Maryland and Texas. And everywhere she went, she impressed people with her skills and athleticism.

In high school, Nykesha immediately became a three-sport standout, a starter as a freshman on the boys' soccer team, an all-league selection in volleyball and an All-American in basketball.

By the time she was a senior, she was scoring more than 36 points per game and was named the National High School Player of the Year. Kids and their parents asked for her autograph, and college coaches from all over the country sent her letters, inviting her to go to their school. The first letter she ever got was from University of Connecticut coach Geno Auriemma.

But she didn't want to go to Connecticut. It was

only 35 minutes away from home, and she wanted to get farther away. But the letters from Coach Auriemma just kept on coming. Finally, she said yes. And it was a good thing, too!

In Nykesha's freshman season, the Huskies won the NCAA title and became the first team in women's college basketball history to go unde-feated. Despite all of the excitement, Nykesha was still adjusting to college life and to the college game.

Nykesha was not a starter, which was a tough thing for a player who'd been the star on every team on which she'd ever played. But the winning made it easier to accept. So did having teammates such as All-Americans Rebecca Lobo, Jennifer Rizzotti and Kara Wolters.

"Winning the national championship as a fresh-man, I didn't really realize what we had done," Nykesha said. "You start to think, 'Hey, this is kind of easy,' but each year we got worse. By the time you are a senior and a team leader, you really want to win again."

Nykesha didn't get the happy ending she was hoping for. She was an All-American, a top pro prospect, and she was about to break the school record for points scored. All she wanted was one more national championship.

RAISE THE ROOF!

Then came February 21, 1998. In a game against Notre Dame, another player stepped on Nykesha's heel. She felt a pop and dropped to the floor. She had never felt so much pain! She knew her college career was over.

Nykesha had ruptured her Achilles tendon, a serious injury that requires surgery and months of rehabilitation. She would not play in the NCAA Tournament or for Connecticut again. And she was just one basket short of the school scoring record.

What happened later in the season made Nykesha famous all over the country. Connecticut was to play Villanova in the season finale. Coach Auriemma called the Villanova coach and arranged for Nykesha to be on the floor at tip-off. Villanova players let Connecticut take the ball and pass it to Nykesha, who was standing under the basket wearing a leg cast. She made the layup for the two points she needed to get the record.

A huge controversy followed. Television, radio stations and newspapers all over the U.S. debated whether Nykesha should have been given the chance to break the record.

"I just tried to keep positive," Nykesha said. "I tried to block out all the talk. I know why we did it, but I respect other people's opinions. People still ask me questions about it, two years later."

While all this was going on, Nykesha's injury began to heal. She had to show up for grueling physical therapy twice a day. She wasn't sure she would get through it. She had to learn how to walk and run again.

It took her five months to return to the court. In the meantime, she'd been named the No. 1 player for the WNBA's Orlando Miracle, one of two expansion teams in the 1998 season. But she could not play because of her injury. She could only watch.

"That was the most frustrating part, because I am such a competitor," Nykesha said. "They were playing and I was doing these little drills, which would have been so simple if I was healthy and I was hardly able to do them."

She was healthy enough in the fall of 1998 to play in an international tour with other WNBA players in Brazil. It took her several games before she could pivot, jump and change directions on her injured foot. But once she did it all, her confidence returned. It was good to be back!

The first season she played in the WNBA was a smashing success. She was the second-leading scorer on the team, averaging 13.7 points and was named to the WNBA All-Star Team. She became an All-Star again in 2000, and led her team in scoring on the way to the playoffs.

"It's fun. The pro game is much faster and you play three and four games a week. You travel east to west and north and south all in one trip," Nykesha said. "But the fans are great and people recognize who you are. I thought that would only happen in college."

Nykesha isn't the only basketball star in her family. Her little brother, Brooks, the one she always had to drag with her to practice and the playground, grew up to be 6-10 and is playing college basketball for Villanova.

"I didn't know he'd grow up to be so big," Nykesha said.

The same can be said for big sister.

Nykesha Sales

Position	Height	Weight	Birth Date	College
Guard	6-0	160	5/10/76	Connecticut '98

Season	Team	G	FG%	FT%	3P%	APG	RPG	SPG	BPG	PPG	PTS
1999	Orlando	32	.385	.805	.330	2.8	4.2	2.16	.25	13.7	437
2000	Orlando	32	.444	.694	.395	2.2	4.3	1.47	.38	13.4	430
Career		64	.414	.767	.364	2.5	4.3	1.81	.31	13.5	867

Did you know

*that Nykesha loves to watch the
soap opera* Guiding Light?

Katie
Smith

It was just a summer ago that Katie Smith ventured down to visit her friend and former teammate Shannon Johnson of the Orlando Miracle in South Carolina.

The two of them pulled on some shorts and laced up their shoes, heading toward the playground for a game of pickup. Katie lives for the chance to play pickup basketball. It reminds her why she loves the game so much. It's not about practicing or lifting weights, or tossing up an endless run of free throws. Pickup ball is just pure competition.

They arrived at the court and declared that they had the next game. The men on the playground looked at Katie doubtfully. Some of them knew Shannon and they knew she could play. But Katie? The country girl who can sew and tap dance sure didn't look like a player. They had no idea that she was a professional, a WNBA All-Star, an Olympian. They had no idea Katie had game. A lot of it!

"It was great," Katie said. "I know I don't look like a baller. But you go there and you drop about five jumpers on them and they figure it out. I love doing that. They still ask about me whenever Shannon goes back there."

When Katie trained and traveled with the U.S. Olympic team, Lisa Leslie, Chamique Holdsclaw and Dawn Staley could never get through the air-port unrecognized. They would always be stopped in the baggage claim signing autographs while Katie would be able to get her bags and wait on the bus.

That would never happen in Ohio. While the Minnesota Lynx star can still walk into her own WNBA arena without being recognized, there aren't many places in Katie's home state she can go without being stopped by fans who have watched her play since she was a kid.

Katie carved out one of the most distinguished athletic careers in Ohio's history. She was a high school standout in her hometown of Logan long before deciding to attend Ohio State. She played more than two years of professional basketball in Columbus, winning two American Basketball League titles with the Columbus Quest. Now she is a two-time WNBA All-Star and was a member of the gold medal-winning 2000 Olympic team.

It's no wonder she can't go to the movies or the grocery store, or even the local amusement park without being recognized by fans and stopped for her autograph. Her mother can't even get out of the grocery store in Logan without other shop-pers—some total strangers—asking about Katie, passing along their good wishes for her success.

"I'd like to have a dollar for every six-year-old named Katie," said Ohio State coach Beth Burns, Katie's college coach. "Katie was a hot name around here in 1993."

Her Ohio fans remember the state championships she won in high school. They remember the 28 points she scored as a freshman in the NCAA Championship game against Texas Tech. They remember the Big Ten career scoring record she set with the Buckeyes.

They remember a player with a versatility that few in the world can match. Katie handles the ball like a guard and possesses the sweetest jump shot. But when she plays under the basket, she is as physical as any player she's defending. She was a post player in high school, and she alternated between guard and forward at Ohio State. Katie is a forward for the Minnesota Lynx, but she played every position on the court for the U.S. team.

"I put her wherever I have to, to keep her on the floor," said U.S. team coach Nell Fortner. "I've played her at center and I've played her at point guard, because there are just times when I can't afford to take her out of the game."

In Minnesota, Katie is the go-to player. The Lynx look for her to score and rebound, and to be a leader on the floor and in the locker room. Katie was the WNBA's second-leading scorer in 2000, averaging more than 20 points per game.

But because Minnesota's games aren't on television as often as Los Angeles, Houston and New York, most WNBA fans haven't seen her play as much as some of the league's other stars.

Katie greets it all with a shrug. She cares more about helping her team than being a star. "Someday, maybe it will happen," Katie said. "I don't worry about it. It's not something I can control."

While Katie seems to be an extraordinary talent, she sees herself as incredibly normal. She's just a kid from the Midwest who grew up on a farm, taking steers and sheep to the fair. She learned how to cook and sew and took ballet and tap-dancing lessons until the seventh grade. But Katie grew up in an athletic-minded family. Her father played college football and her mother was a swimmer.

And by the time Katie hung up her tap shoes, she was more interested in basketball than anything else.

Katie was in fifth grade when she played in her first basketball game on an all-boys team called the Bobcats. She was one of the tallest players on the team, taller even than her older brother, who was also on the team.

By the time Katie was a sixth-grader, she was

playing on girls teams in Logan, traveling around the state for games. She would marvel at the number of girls playing in these tournaments. Her parents would also take her to women's basketball games at Ohio State University, where they had both gone to college. Katie would sit in the stands, watch the games and wonder: "How did these girls get to play basketball in college?"

Katie's questions were answered when the recruiting letters began showing up in her mailbox as early as seventh grade.

Ohio State was among the schools sending letters. And Katie knew that she wanted to stay close to home after high school to play college ball.

"I wanted my family to see me play, but I also wanted the people that watched me grow up to have a chance to follow me," Katie said. "I have a lot of history with the people here."

Katie's freshman season was a huge success. Her team reached the NCAA title game against Sheryl Swoopes' team, falling just short with an 84–82 loss. The Buckeyes never went back to the title game, but Katie had one of the best careers in NCAA history, finishing with 2,578 points.

Fortunately for both Katie and her Ohio fans, she would get to begin her professional career in familiar territory as well, playing for the ABL's

Columbus Quest. The Quest was the most dominant team in the short history of the ABL, winning
both titles, and Katie was a large part of the reason
why. The Quest was off to another strong start in
the 1998 season when Katie injured her knee. A
couple of days later, Katie was named as one of the
core players to the 2000 Olympic team. She was
relieved.

"If I hadn't made the Olympic team, there would
have been a lot of pressure to get back, maybe
before my knee was ready," Katie said. "But it gave
me a lot of peace of mind."

That peace of mind was gone just a few weeks
later, when the ABL folded. Katie wasn't sure what
her basketball future held. It turns out she had little to worry about. Katie was assigned to the
Minnesota Lynx, where she would play for former
Quest coach Brian Agler. Her knee was nearly
healed by the time the season began, but still it was
a difficult one.

That knee is completely healed now and Katie is
as confident in her game as ever.

"I might not get hounded or mobbed like some
of the other players," Katie said. "But I can sit back
and know that I am just as good as anyone."

Just ask the guys on that court in South
Carolina.

Katie Smith

Position	Height	Weight	Birth Date	College
Forward	5-11	181	6/4/74	Ohio State '96

Season	Team	G	FG%	FT%	3P%	APG	RPG	SPG	BPG	PPG	PTS
1999	Minnesota	30	.387	.766	.382	2.0	2.9	.63	.33	11.7	350
2000	Minnesota	32	.421	.869	.379	2.8	2.9	1.38	.22	20.2	646
Career		62	.408	.833	.380	2.4	2.9	1.02	.27	16.1	996

Did you know
that Katie began taking
tap-dancing lessons when she
was just four years old?

Dawn Staley

Every day, when Dawn Staley takes the court, she wears a rubber band on her right wrist. And every time she commits a turnover, she snaps herself. No pain, no gain!

When Dawn was a girl, challenging bigger, stronger kids on the playgrounds in Philadelphia, she wanted to be like her NBA hero, Philadelphia 76ers star point guard Maurice "Mo" Cheeks, the player who originally came up with the rubber band idea.

It worked for him and it's worked for her. Now Dawn—all five feet, six inches of her—is a role model in Philadelphia as well.

If she couldn't already tell she was a hero because people stopped to talk to her on the street or by the fact that her high school named their gymnasium in her honor, she knew the moment she looked up onto a seven-story downtown Philadelphia building and saw a giant mural with her photo painted on the bricks.

"The wall wasn't really a dream of mine," said Staley on the day it was unveiled. "You don't dream of yourself on a seven-story building. You dream about making an Olympic team. Graduating from high school. Graduating from college. But to see yourself on a seven-story mural is really incredible and really overwhelming."

Dawn has established herself as one of the most skilled and well-respected players in the world. As a star point guard for the WNBA's Charlotte Sting and two gold-medal winning U.S. Olympic teams, she combines the flash of the no-look pass and the between-the-legs dribble with the leadership skills and court demeanor of an experienced veteran player.

Legendary point guard Magic Johnson and NBA All-Star Gary Payton count themselves among her biggest fans. Former Philadelphia 76ers coach John Lucas called her the best point guard in the city. The opinion of Magic Johnson, one of the best guards ever to play the game, means a lot to Dawn.

"The fact that he plays the same position and understands the game as well as anybody whose played at his level," Dawn said. "A lot of people give you compliments, but coming from Magic it's a great honor."

The youngest of five children, and nearly always the smallest one out on the playground, Dawn was an unlikely basketball star. At first, her brothers brought her to pickup games because they had to, and protected her because they thought they needed to.

Then came the day when Dawn became the only girl chosen to play pickup with the guys. She didn't need their help anymore!

"She came home only to eat and sleep," said Dawn's mother, Estelle.

Estelle Staley cleaned houses every weekday to support her kids. Most of the rest of the time that she wasn't at home she spent at the local Baptist church, where she sang.

But Estelle managed to keep close watch on her kids. Life in the housing projects of North Philadelphia could be dangerous. Drugs and guns were as common on the playgrounds as the pick-up games in which Dawn was constantly playing. She played for hours every day, even when, as her brother Eric said, "We tried to send her home, but she wouldn't go."

Dawn calls her mother her biggest inspiration. "She allowed me to go out and play with the guys when a lot of mothers wouldn't have allowed their seven-or eight-year-old to continue to do it," Dawn said with admiration. "But we didn't live that far from the basketball court. It wasn't exactly shouting distance, but somehow I always heard her when she told me to bring my butt back in the house. And when she used my middle name, she was serious."

Dawn began playing organized basketball in elementary school. She was often the only girl in the league. In high school at Dobbins Tech, Dawn used the game as refuge for her troubles. If she was disappointed or upset, she would play. It always made her feel better.

Dawn was a high school star. She led her team on a 60-game winning streak and three city championships. It was enough to earn her a scholarship at the University of Virginia.

Dawn's transition to college was difficult. In her freshman season at Virginia, she struggled in the classroom and needed tutors to help improve her grades. On the court she was constantly plagued with turnovers. It was then that she put on the rubber band.

"Mo was my favorite player in the game. I remember seeing the story in the paper about what he did and I thought it would work well for me," Dawn said. "I was averaging like five turnovers a game at the time. The rubber band was a disciplinary tool for me."

And it worked like a charm!

Dawn led her team to a record of 110 wins and 21 losses, with three trips to the NCAA Final Four and one national championship game. She was named the national Player of the Year in 1991 and 1992. She became just one of three players in Virginia's school history to have her jersey retired.

After college, Dawn knew she would have to go

overseas if she wanted to continue her career. It was the path that so many other talented American players had taken. But it wasn't easy for any of them.

By the time she returned home to play for the U.S. Olympic team in 1995, Dawn had played in Brazil, Italy, Spain and France.

Dawn called those three years overseas "lonely and humbling." She swore she'd never get on another plane and cross the ocean to play ball. But within a year, Dawn was headed around the world with the U.S. National Team to prepare for the 1996 Olympic Games in Atlanta. One year later, when she stood on the podium and the gold medal was draped around her neck, Dawn called it "the greatest basketball moment in my life."

During the exhausting months of travel with the Olympic team, it was Dawn who kept her teammates entertained. She hosted movie parties and took one-dollar bets on whose suitcase would come off the baggage carousel first. She's the one who always won the card games with playing partner and best friend Lisa Leslie.

And she's the one who organized her teammates into donating clothes and sneakers to the players on the Cuban National Team.

She's made helping others a theme in her life and career. Dawn started the Dawn Staley Foundation in Philadelphia, which supports summer basketball leagues, after-school programs and activities for kids. Her goal is to build a recreation center in Philadelphia.

"The foundation is exceeding everything I thought it could be," Dawn said. "I'm happy to give kids the opportunity to have a fresh start, learn computers, play basketball, whatever they need."

Dawn's days in the WNBA have been good and bad. She led her team to the playoffs in the 1999 season, but Charlotte struggled in 2000, winning only eight games in the entire season. Losing is difficult for Dawn, but she has never been discouraged from giving her best effort. That's why she is such a great leader.

"I think we are all disappointed in our record," Dawn explained. "But we aren't disappointed with the effort we gave night in, night out. That's what impressed me most, that we have all stayed positive."

Dawn's basketball career has extended beyond the limits of a player recently, as well. She was hired in 2000 as the head coach at Temple University in her hometown of Philadelphia. Dawn is thrilled to be returning to the place where her career began. She will continue her playing career as she starts on a new journey as a coach.

"To come back here as a coach is a truly awesome experience," Dawn said the day she was hired. "A lot of people question my experience as a coach and only time will answer that."

Someday, Dawn hopes to be the general manager of a WNBA team.

Dawn has known great success, and has battled

adversity, including several injuries to her knees that have required surgery and time away from the game. But Dawn is undaunted in achieving her goals.

"I believe that if you set goals and you achieve them, it helps you reach out further the next time," Staley said. "After a while it snowballs into something really big."

Like a seven-story building.

Dawn Staley

Position	Height	Weight	Birth Date	College
Guard	5-6	134	5/4/70	Virginia '92

Season	Team	G	FG%	FT%	3P%	APG	RPG	SPG	BPG	PPG	PTS
1999	Charlotte	32	.415	.934	.317	5.5	2.3	1.19	.09	11.5	368
2000	Charlotte	32	.372	.878	.330	5.9	2.4	1.16	.03	8.8	282
Career		64	.395	.909	.323	5.7	2.3	1.17	.06	10.2	650

Did you know
*that Dawn sits in a cold
whirlpool before every game
to get herself fired up?*

Tina Thompson

"Showtime" was always family time for Tina Thompson and her family. All seven people, Tina, her parents, her two brothers and two sisters would gather around the television regularly to watch Los Angeles Lakers games.

Game night was always a special night. Dinner didn't have to be eaten in the kitchen, but was brought into the den instead. Everyone took their regular places on the floor to watch the team that won five NBA Championships in the 1980s. A team that was playing right down the road at the Great Western Forum in Tina's hometown of Inglewood.

"We all cheered and yelled," Tina said about watching Lakers' games. "It was a very special time."

Tina's family still gathers to watch championship basketball. But this time it's the Houston Comets.

Tina is one of the most decorated players in the WNBA, having earned four WNBA Championship rings with Houston. And while Tina doesn't have league Most Valuable Player Awards like teammates Cynthia Cooper and Sheryl Swoopes, she is no less valuable to the Comets' success.

Tina is one of the toughest players in the world at her position. She rebounds. She defends. And then she draws bigger, slower players out to the perimeter, where she makes them pay by burying three-pointers. Tina has become such a dominant force that she was named MVP of the 2000 WNBA All-Star Game.

"Tina gets mentioned, but not enough," said Sheryl Swoopes. "I'm proud of her and proud for her."

Truth be told, as a 10-year-old girl, Tina didn't really want to play basketball. She hadn't really been interested in any sports, other than cheerleading. And she had few examples to follow.

"There weren't very many girls in my neighborhood playing sports," Tina said.

But basketball was a good excuse to follow her older brother Tommy to the playground or the recreation center.

"I always said I wanted to play, but the truth was, I didn't have that much interest," Tina said. But after enduring constant rejection and put-downs by her brother and his friends, she became very interested in proving them wrong.

"I wanted to show them that girls could play, and then I started to have a lot of fun," Tina said.

Tina was 13 when she joined the same recreational team as her brother. She was the only girl and did not play much. Usually, Tina didn't get on to the court until the score got so lopsided the coach figured she couldn't cost her team the game.

And then came the day that Tina and Tommy's team faced a desperate situation. With only six players available and one of them fouled out, Tina would have to play with the game on the line.

Tina ended up with the ball. With all of her teammates screaming for her to pass, she took the game-winning shot. And it went in!

"None of them had any idea I was going to make it," Tina said. "I shot the ball really confidently and when I made it I acted like I was the only one who wasn't surprised. But I really was."

But Tommy and his friends began to treat her differently.

"He told me he thought it was pretty brave to take that shot," Tina remembered. "After that, he assisted me a lot more, rather than just being critical."

Tommy saw the talent in his little sister and he wanted her to get serious. He wanted her to practice hard and be consistent. He wanted her to be good.

He got his wish.

Tina was both a hard worker and a very talented basketball player. After a while, Tina didn't make much room for anything else in her life, even when she got to high school.

"I was very serious. I didn't go to slumber parties or dances and I didn't hang out at the mall unless someone in my family was going," Tina said. "Basketball was what I did and I did it all the time."

Tina had dreams of going to law school. She was about halfway through her high school career when she realized she could earn a scholarship to college.

"When I knew that I could go to school for free, I began to practice even more," Tina said. And recruiters were certainly interested in Tina. She would get six to eight letters a day. More than thirty coaches visited her home, trying to convince her to come to their school.

Tina finally chose the University of Southern California because of her overwhelming desire to stay close to home. She didn't even consider schools that weren't on the West Coast.

"I wanted my family to be able to watch me play," Tina said.

Tina was recruited by one coach and played for two others during her four years at USC. One of those coaches was Cheryl Miller, who is considered one of the greatest women's basketball players of all time. Tina was inspired by Coach Miller's example.

"She's an absolutely great motivator. She has a way with words that's unbelievable," Tina said. Miller helped inspire Tina on her way to a spectac-

ular college career. Tina finished her career as the Pac-10's third-leading career scorer and second-leading career rebounder.

There was little doubt Tina would become a professional basketball player in the WNBA. Tina hoped that she might be drafted by the Los Angeles Sparks, which would offer her more chances to play close to home. Instead, Tina was chosen as the first draft pick in WNBA history by the Houston Comets. That worked out pretty well, too. Tina has ended every WNBA season with a championship celebration.

"It would have been a blessing to play at home, but I wouldn't change a thing now," Tina said. "We have made our own history in Houston."

Winning has never grown commonplace for Tina. There is still no better feeling than standing in the middle of the court with the crowd cheering and the balloons and confetti falling from the rafters.

"It never gets old," she said simply.

But there have been tough times in Houston as well. Tina and her Comet teammates are still getting over the death of their team's point guard, Kim Perrot. Perrot was diagnosed with lung cancer in the months before the 1999 season and passed away at the age of 32 just before the 1999 Playoffs began. The Comets were forced to play a game the

day after Kim's death. They lost to Los Angeles 68-64 in that game. Tina scored 13 points and spent much of the game wiping away the tears rolling down her face.

Tina was very close to Kim and her death was a devastating blow.

"It was like losing a member of my family," Tina said. "We were very close. I talked with her as much as any of my teammates, not just about basketball, but about everything. Losing Kim is something I'm still getting over. It hasn't gone away yet, and I don't think it ever will."

But Tina has much to look forward to. She isn't sure how long her WNBA career will last. At some point, she says, she might walk away. She still dreams of going to law school. Eventually, she wants to become a judge.

"I know I have at least three or four more years of basketball in me," Tina vowed. And she certainly has room left on her hands for a few more rings!

Tina Thompson

Position	Height	Weight	Birth Date	College
Forward	6-2	178	2/10/75	Univ. Southern California '97

Season	Team	G	FG%	FT%	3P%	APG	RPG	SPG	BPG	PPG	PTS
1997	Houston	28	.418	.838	.370	1.1	6.6	0.75	1.00	13.2	370
1998	Houston	27	.419	.851	.359	0.9	7.1	1.15	.93	12.7	342
1999	Houston	32	.419	.782	.351	0.9	6.4	.97	.97	12.2	391
2000	Houston	32	.469	.837	.417	1.5	7.7	1.47	.78	16.9	540
Career		119	.434	.827	.377	1.1	6.9	1.09	.92	13.8	1,643

Did you know

*that Tina wears the same color lipstick,
called "Diva," during every game she plays?*

Teresa Weatherspoon

People still talk about The Shot. Teresa Weatherspoon gets asked about it all the time. "How long was it?" "Did you think you were going to make it?" "Is it the great accomplishment in your career?" She's answered all the questions.

Teresa Weatherspoon has been one of the most well-known, well-respected players in the WNBA from the day she played for the New York Liberty in the league's first-ever game against Los Angeles in June of 1997. She has appeared on *The Rosie O'Donnell Show* and *Late Night with David Letterman.* Her distinctive braids have made her recognizable virtually every where she goes.

But when "T-Spoon" threw up a shot from behind the half-court line as the buzzer sounded in Game 2 of the 1999 WNBA Championships to beat the reigning champion Houston Comets, she became famous in ways she never could have imagined. It was incredible!

The play was shown on television for days. It turned out to be one of the greatest moments in league history. Houston ended up winning its third WNBA title, but Teresa's shot will be the thing about that series that people will never forget.

"I don't mind talking about it," Teresa said. "But that shot is not what made me as a player. It was a lot of hard work and effort."

There isn't a player in all of the league who would argue that. Teresa wins everywhere she goes. She took Louisiana Tech to two NCAA Final Fours and an NCAA Championship. She has taken the New York Liberty on three trips to the WNBA Championships. Sometimes she has done it with her scoring and her assists. Other times she has done it with sheer will, with her arms waving in the air, exciting both the crowd and her teammates.

Liberty general manager Carol Blazejowski, who is a legendary player in her own right, calls Teresa "clearly the heart and the soul of the Liberty."

And if one basketball coach hadn't decided to take a ride deep into Texas, perhaps no one would have ever known about her. Pineland, Texas, isn't a place people visit regularly. Only 800 people live there and not many others pass through town.

"It's not a city, or even a town, it's a crack," Teresa joked.

But it's a good thing for women's basketball that Louisiana Tech coach Leon Barmore read the map and found his way there.

At the gymnasium at West Sabine High School, Coach Barmore watched Teresa play. By halftime he knew he had found a player who was exactly what his team needed. The girl from that small town had big-time game!

She was an exceptional talent and an emotional fireplug. She drew a crowd to high school games long before women's basketball's popularity had exploded at the college level. All of these people must have known they were seeing something special whenever Teresa played.

"Teresa had that gym packed and filled with excitement," Coach Barmore remembered. "She was just an incredible athlete, and played with such unbelievable enthusiasm. People came out just for the chance to see her play."

The youngest of six children, Teresa's first experience with basketball came when she followed her older brothers to the sandlot across the street. Playing basketball was one of the few things there was for the kids to do in Pinewood.

Her older brothers, Charles Jr. and Michael, would let her play, but the boys in the game gave her no breaks. She was not as big as most of them and they let her know it by blocking her shots and knocking her around.

She figured out a way to solve her height problem by working on the other parts of her game: ball-handling, passing and defense.

"It took me a while to be able to play with them,

TERESA WEATHERSPOON

but when I did it, I had no problems," Teresa said.

Teresa played both basketball and baseball, which were the only two sports available to her.

"I was eleven years old. I would have done anything and enjoyed it," Teresa said. She always played like she loved it.

Coach Barmore brought Teresa to Louisiana Tech's campus in Ruston, Louisiana, in the fall of 1983. Teresa was homesick for a while.

"I was Momma's baby, you know," she said. But Teresa began to fit in with the team immediately. She was just 18 years old and already the starting point guard for one of the top teams in the nation. She played like a veteran. In March of the 1984–85 season, in a game that would determine her team's place in the NCAA Tournament, Weatherspoon hit another one of those big shots.

It came against the USC Trojans, the two-time defending national champions. It was a long jumper that tied the game and sent it into overtime. Louisiana Tech eventually won 83–79.

"Here I was this little freshman with Cheryl Miller playing on the other team, and that play wasn't even designed for me, but I hit the shot," Teresa said. "That was my turning point. It was the point at which I knew I could play with anybody."

The statistics prove her right.

Over the course of her four-year career, Teresa led Louisiana Tech to 118 wins and the 1988 NCAA Championship. At the end of that season she was named the top collegiate women's player. She still holds school records in assists and steals.

After her college career ended, Teresa moved on to bigger things, playing for the 1988 Olympic team that won a gold medal in Seoul. After the Olympics, Teresa began an eight-year professional career overseas. She played in Italy for six years, twice making the Italian League All-Star team, then played in Russia for two years.

In the meantime, she again represented the United States on the 1992 Olympic team that won a bronze medal. It would still be another four long years before the opportunity to play professionally in the United States came to be.

When she did join the Liberty, Teresa, a 31-year-old veteran, wasn't as well known as the Liberty's star player, Rebecca Lobo. Rebecca had recently been the star of the Connecticut team that won the national title in 1995. That team introduced women's basketball to the entire nation and Rebecca became a household name.

Teresa wasn't yet a household name, just a player with a lot of experience. It turned out the Liberty needed just that. New York played in the

RAISE THE ROOF!

title game the first season and, after missing the playoffs in 1998, returned to the Championships in both 1999 and 2000. Teresa, leading the team, has twice been named the WNBA's Defensive Player of the Year and has led the league in steals twice.

New York and Teresa seem to be a perfect fit. Her intensity, emotion and gutty play have been well received by New Yorkers who consider Madison Square Garden to be one of the most legendary basketball venues in the world.

Teresa has gone from being just a basketball player to a role model.

"Once you get that label, it's on you," Teresa said. "I put it on my shoulders and I carry it. It's a good thing. Kids need to see positive things."

Teresa will be 35 when the 2001 season begins. She will be one of the oldest players in the league and is already looking ahead to the day when she will play her last game. As she left the court after Louisiana Tech won the NCAA title in 1988, she knew she had given it everything she had.

"That is how I want to walk away from the WNBA. That is how I'd like to be remembered."

Teresa Weatherspoon

Position	Height	Weight	Birth Date	College
Guard	5-8	161	12/8/65	Louisiana Tech '88

Season	Team	G	FG%	FT%	3P%	APG	RPG	SPG	BPG	PPG	PTS
1997	New York	28	.467	.650	.086	6.1	4.1	3.04	.07	7.0	196
1998	New York	30	.388	.609	.327	6.4	4.0	3.33	.00	6.8	204
1999	New York	32	.421	.679	.378	6.4	3.3	2.44	.09	7.2	229
2000	New York	32	.438	.741	.250	6.4	3.4	2.03	.16	6.4	205
Career		122	.425	.670	.290	6.3	3.7	2.69	.08	6.8	834

Did you know
that Teresa not only wears No. 11,
but also wears 11 braids in her hair?

Natalie Williams

It's funny how things work out. Natalie Williams has always seemed destined for the Olympics. But after devoting her life for a year and a half to the U.S. Olympic volleyball team, she was the last player cut from the roster before the team left for Atlanta in 1996.

Natalie was more disappointed than she'd ever been in her life. She sat on the couch in her apartment in Long Beach, California, crying as she watched the Opening Ceremonies. She also felt tired, feeling she had finally had enough of the sport she'd played since seventh grade. Natalie wanted to try pursuing something else. That something else turned out to be much better.

Four years later, Natalie was wearing the red, white and blue—for the U.S. Olympic women's basketball team. One way or another, Natalie was going to get her medal.

"Getting cut from the volleyball team, maybe it was the best thing that happened to me," Natalie said.

Natalie, a two-time WNBA All-Star with the Utah Starzz, is a world-class athlete in two sports, which is a testament to her versatility and tremendous physical gifts. Her quickness, agility and impressive jumping ability make her one of the best power forwards in the world. But she is also a strong, physical player with the will to work hard and a nose for rebounds. Natalie is a complete package.

It has been clear since she was a young child that her athletic talent was as big as her frequent smile. As an eight-year-old girl, Natalie was knocking softballs over fences, which her teammates could do only if they ran to the fence and threw the ball over.

In high school, her best friend—one of Utah's top high school track athletes—taught Natalie how to long jump. On her first try, Natalie broke the state record.

"God gives people good voices and they're singers," said U.S. Olympic basketball coach Nell Fortner. "God blessed [Natalie] with an incredible amount of athletic ability. I've never seen anyone who could jump so high from a standing position."

Looking at Natalie, who stands six feet, two inches tall, it's hard to believe she was ever small enough to fit in a drawer. But that's the way she traveled from Long Beach, where she was born, to her new home in Utah, with her mother, Robyn. They didn't have a car seat.

Natalie grew up in Utah, a biracial child in a community where there weren't many people who looked like her.

"I didn't really know any different," Natalie said.

"The biggest thing in Utah is that I think I changed a lot of people's views on minorities."

Natalie remembers getting called names when she started elementary school, but that quickly stopped.

"Everybody got used to the fact that I was just Nat."

Nat's athletic career began at the age of eight when she began playing softball. She loved the sport, but as she grew rapidly in strength and size, people started suggesting she play basketball. By junior high, she was a head taller than all of the girls and most of the boys.

Hoops was in her blood, after all. Natalie's father was a former basketball player who had played in the NBA for eight years. But Natalie didn't know her father then. She did not meet him until she was 16. Natalie began playing volleyball in the seventh grade, but did not play her first basketball game until the eighth grade.

Her junior high school basketball coach, Sandy Catten, saw Natalie's potential. She put her in a jump-training program to help Natalie hone her leaping ability. It worked like a charm!

Natalie had a trophy-filled high school career at Taylorsville High School, and won state championships in both basketball and volleyball.

She was heavily recruited in both sports. There were so many letters from coaches that her head would spin just trying to sort through them all. UCLA was one of the schools that wanted Natalie. But Natalie didn't want to go to UCLA, and had already turned down UCLA's invitation to visit the campus on a recruiting trip. Instead, she agreed to go down the road in Los Angeles to visit USC. As part of that visit, she went with USC coaches to the UCLA campus to see a game against the Bruins.

As soon as she saw the UCLA campus, Natalie knew she had made a mistake.

"I just fell in love with the whole surroundings and I called UCLA back the next week and said 'You know, I think I'll take my trip now,'" Natalie remembered.

Natalie had little trouble balancing both sports while at UCLA. She had been doing it for years. She had little trouble succeeding at both of them, either. In volleyball, she was twice named the National Player of the Year and was a four-time All-American. She led UCLA to two NCAA titles and four trips to the Final Four.

In basketball, Natalie was a two-time All-American. She set the Pac-10 Conference record for the highest rebound average (12.8 per game) and was the 1994 Pac-10 Player of the Year.

RAISE THE ROOF!

Natalie ended up having one of the finest athletic careers in collegiate sports history, becoming the first woman to be an All-American in two sports in the same school year.

Unfortunately, she also ended up injured. A knee injury ended her senior basketball season a few weeks early. She then had to work hard to get in shape for the U.S. volleyball team. As she had always done, Natalie did the work. And she spent 18 months with the volleyball team, doing everything she could to make sure she would be on the Olympic roster. And then she wasn't.

"I was just ready for something new," Natalie remembered. "I was burned out with everything that had happened, and training so hard and having a letdown. I thought, 'Let me go and do something I really, really enjoy.'"

Basketball was the perfect choice. Before she knew it, Natalie was on a plane to Taiwan, representing the U.S. in the Jones Cup tournament. The team won the gold medal. Later that year, Natalie signed with the American Basketball League and began playing for the Portland Power.

Anyone who had forgotten what a great basketball player Natalie was got a very quick reminder. Natalie was named the ABL's Most Valuable Player in 1998.

Natalie was eventually chosen as part of the 1998 World Championship Team, which also won a gold medal. When the ABL folded later that year, everyone knew that Natalie would be one of the top picks in the WNBA Draft.

She was thrilled when Utah took her with the No. 3 pick. It was her chance to go home!

"I really didn't know it would ever be possible, but it was something I'd always dreamt about, playing back home in front of all my family and friends," Natalie said. "I feel like I never left, even though I was gone nearly ten years." Natalie came home as a professional basketball player. *Only* a basketball player.

Natalie bought her first home in Utah. Her three cats, Torby, Tricity and Grizzly, have more room to roam than they did in her old apartments.

Her relationship with her father has developed so much that he now gives her frequent advice, sometimes whether she wants it or not.

"You know how fathers are," Natalie said with a laugh. "Always putting their two cents in. He tries to help. But he has offered me a lot of good insight about being a professional athlete and what areas of my game I need to keep strong."

It would seem Natalie already knows that part. Just ask her old ABL coach Lin Dunn.

"Natalie may turn out to be somebody like Bill Russell or Wilt Chamberlain, where we will look at her as one of the most dominant players in the history of our game."

Natalie Williams

Position **Height** **Weight** **Birth Date** **College**
Forward 6-2 217 11/30/70 UCLA '92

Season	Team	G	FG%	FT%	3P%	APG	RPG	SPG	BPG	PPG	PTS
1999	Utah	28	.519	.754	.000	0.9	9.2	1.36	.79	18.0	504
2000	Utah	29	.490	.798	.600	1.8	11.6	1.21	.62	18.7	543
Career		57	.504	.778	.429	1.3	10.4	1.28	.70	18.4	1,047

Did you know
that Natalie is a huge
Harry Potter fan?